Dear Parent:

Congratulations! Your child is taking the first steps on an exciting journey. The destination? Independent reading!

STEP INTO READING® will help your child get there. The program offers books at five levels that accompany children from their first attempts at reading to reading success. Each step includes fun stories, fiction and nonfiction, and colorful art. There are also Step into Reading Sticker Books, Step into Reading Math Readers, and Step into Reading Phonics Readers— a complete literacy program with something to interest every child.

Learning to Read, Step by Step!

Ready to Read   Preschool–Kindergarten
• big type and easy words • rhyme and rhythm • picture clues
For children who know the alphabet and are eager to begin reading.

Reading with Help   Preschool–Grade 1
• basic vocabulary • short sentences • simple stories
For children who recognize familiar words and sound out new words with help.

Reading on Your Own   Grades 1–3
• engaging characters • easy-to-follow plots • popular topics
For children who are ready to read on their own.

Reading Paragraphs   Grades 2–3
• challenging vocabulary • short paragraphs • exciting stories
For newly independent readers who read simple sentences with confidence.

Ready for Chapters   Grades 2–4
• chapters • longer paragraphs • full-color art
For children who want to take the plunge into chapter books but still like colorful pictures.

STEP INTO READING® is designed to give every child a successful reading experience. The grade levels are only guides. Children can progress through the steps at their own speed, developing confidence in their reading, no matter what their grade.

Remember, a lifetime love of reading starts with a single step!

*To my mom & dad (Bill & Mary),
the original Mommy & Daddy Dinky Doos!
Thank you for not painting over the drawing
I did on the radiator in my room.*

Special thanks to Katonah and Lewisboro Elementary Schools

Photography by Sandra Kress

Clean-up and inking by Vinh Truong

Digital coloring and compositing by Paul Zdanowicz

Copyright © 2006 by Cartoon Pizza, Inc., and Sesame Workshop. PINKY DINKY DOO and associated characters, trademarks, and design elements are owned and licensed by Cartoon Pizza, Inc., and Sesame Workshop. Sesame Workshop and its logos are trademarks and service marks of Sesame Workshop. All rights reserved. Published in the United States by Random House Children's Books, a division of Random House, Inc., New York, and in Canada by Random House of Canada Limited, Toronto, in conjunction with Sesame Workshop.

STEP INTO READING, RANDOM HOUSE, and the Random House colophon are registered trademarks of Random House, Inc.

www.stepintoreading.com

Educators and librarians, for a variety of teaching tools, visit us at
www.randomhouse.com/teachers

Library of Congress Cataloging-in-Publication Data
Jinkins, Jim.
Pinky Dinky Doo : Think pink! / by Jim Jinkins.
    p. cm. — (Step into reading. Step 3 book)
SUMMARY: Pinky Dinky Doo, an imaginative young girl, tells her brother a story about the day when her hair turned pink.
ISBN 0-375-83573-3 (trade) — ISBN 0-375-93573-8 (lib. bdg.)
[1. Change—Fiction. 2. Hair—Fiction. 3. Brothers and sisters—Fiction. 4. Imagination—Fiction. 5. Storytelling—Fiction.] I. Title. II. Series.
PZ7.J57526Pho 2006 [E]—dc22 2005011669

Printed in the United States of America 10 9 8 7 6 5 4 3 2 1 First Edition

STEP INTO READING®

STEP 3

Pinky Dinky Doo™

THINK PINK!

by Jim Jinkins

Random House 🏠 New York

Mr. Guinea Pig

Tyler Doo

Mommy Doo

Daddy Doo

Pinky Dinky Doo

Nicholas Biscuit

Daffinee Toilette

Bobby Boom

Abby McTabby

Lane Puppytray

Ross Applesauce

"New pajamas!"

cried Pinky.

"Oh no!

Let's call the pajama police!"

"Not funny,"
said Tyler.
"I liked my
old pajamas
with the face
on them.
These are different.
These are not
my favorites."

"You don't like things to change,
do you?"
asked Pinky.

Tyler shook his head.

Pinky, you've changed.

"But,
     Tyler,"
  Pinky said,
"sometimes change
  can be good.
  Change can be a
  Pinky Dinky Do."
"No!"
  Tyler said.

"Change is a Pinky Dinky Don't!"

Which of these are Pinky Dinky Do's
and which are Pinky Dinky Don'ts?

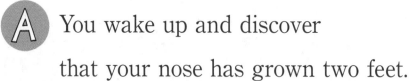

A You wake up and discover
that your nose has grown two feet.

Don't.

Unless you walk
on your face!

B You discover that your
glass of lemonade
is half empty.

A definite
don't.

Full

$\frac{1}{2}$

Empty

Unless it's
also half full.

"I think I see what you mean,"
said Tyler.

"Change can be good or bad."

It just depends on how you look at it.

All this talk about change
gave Pinky an idea.
"Do you want to hear
one of my made-up stories?"
she asked.

"Okay,"

said Pinky.

"I'll just shut my eyes,

wiggle my ears,

and crank up my imagination."

The name of this story is . . .

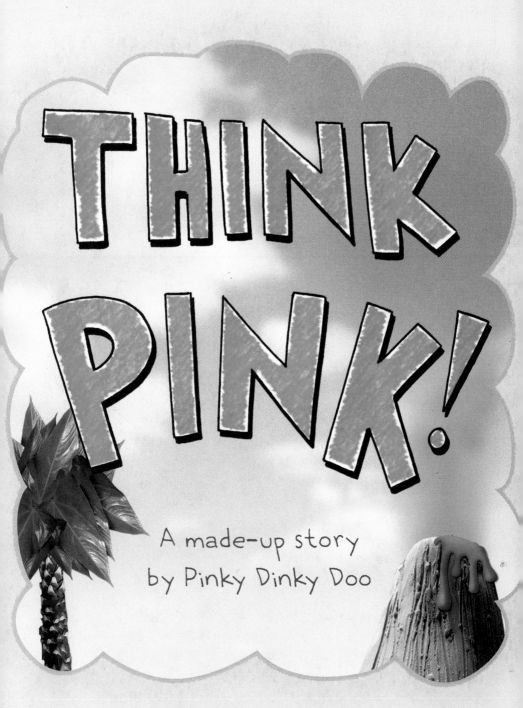

THINK PINK!

A made-up story
by Pinky Dinky Doo

One day in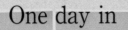
Great Big City,
Pinky woke up,
looked in the
bathroom mirror,
and BAM!

She discovered that
her hair had turned PINK!

It was not pinkish.

It was not pink-like.

It was hot,

bright

pinky-pink-pink!

Yes,

Pinky's name

was Pinky.

But her hair

was supposed

to be yellow.

Even worse,

Pinky hated the color

So Pinky:

A Called 911 and reported

a hair emergency.

B Covered up the pink
with whipped cream
and put a cherry
on top.

C Went to find Mommy Doo . . .

fast!

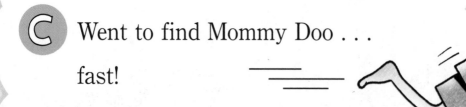

As usual,

the answer was  C .

Mommy Doo patted Pinky's pink head.

She gave her a great big hug.

Then she took out a photo album.

. . . Great-Grandma Doo

lived in a lovely cave.

In one quick second,
the giant beast gobbled up
all of Great-Grandma Doo's
prehistoric cave muffins.

She tried everything to get rid of
the uninvited guest.
She ignored him.

But he just ate her newspaper.

She banged some pots together
to try to scare him away.

But he just ate the pots.

Then Great-Grandma Doo
got really,

really angry.

So she decided to

Think Big.

Normally, Great-Grandma Doo
had an everyday,
prehistoric,
great-grandma-sized brain.
But when she used it
to Think Big,

her head grew

and grew

until it filled the whole cave.
Great-Grandma floated outside.

'Wow!'

she exclaimed.

'Look at that volcano!

Look at that saber-toothed
guinea pig family running away
from the bright red lava.'

And then . . .

Great-Grandma Doo

had a big idea!

'I know what to do!

I'll just . . .

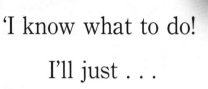 **A** Turn myself into great-grandma stew.

Nah—too salty.

B Pack up and move away.

Hmm . . . I can't wait until somebody invents the TV.

C Make my hair as red as
that lava and scare away
that mean old guinea pig.'

The answer was **C**, of course. And Great-Grandma Doo's lava red hair really did scare the saber-toothed guinea pig.

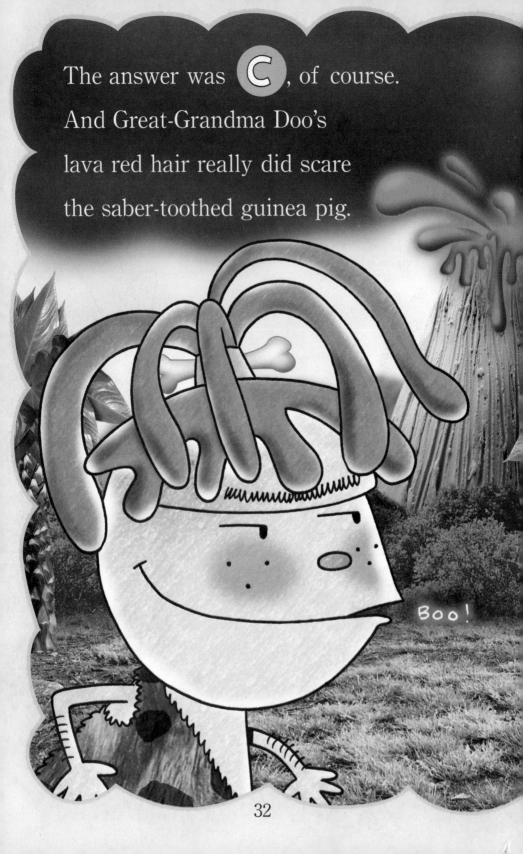

Boo!

It scared him so much
that his giant teeth fell right out
of his mouth and he shrank
to the size of a cave squirrel.

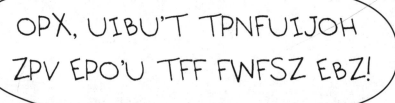

There is a trick for decoding cave language. Can you figure out what Great-Grandma Doo said?

Here's a hint from Professor Pinky:

Each letter in cave language

stands for the one BEFORE it in ours.

Example: Z = A   C = D

A = B   D = E

B = C   E = F

Etc.

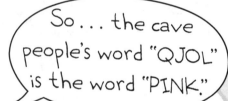

So ... the cave people's word "QJOL" is the word "PINK."

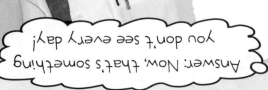

Answer: Now, that's something you don't see every day!

"Great-Grandma Doo decided that she really liked her new red lava hair.

She realized that she liked
her new friend,
the squirrel-sized
guinea pig, too.

So she invited him for lunch
and they ate delicious prehistoric
grilled cheese sandwiches.

And from that day on,
when anyone in
the Doo family
decided to Think Big,
there was a good chance that
their hair might change color."

The End.

"And that's *exactly* what happened,"
said Pinky.
"Sort of."

"But, P-P-Pinky!"
cried Tyler.
"Your hair really did
turn PINK!"

"Wow,
little brother!"
said Pinky.

"You're right!
My hair changed
just like
Great-Grandma
Doo's did!"

"I think I like my pink hair,"
said Pinky Dinky Doo.
"At least for now."

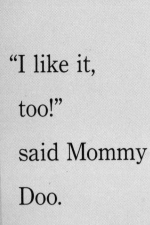

"I like it,
too!"
said Mommy
Doo.

"It shows that you really do

Think Big.

And pink is one of my favorite colors."

Tyler thought really hard.

"Hmm,

maybe change *can* be good,"

he said.

And because now
Tyler was Thinking Big,
his hair
suddenly
turned
blue!

Cool!

"Yay,

change!"

cheered Pinky.

"Come on,

little blue-haired brother.

Let's show off our brand-new

colored do's to Daddy Doo."

"Last one downstairs

is a prehistoric cave muffin!"

Later that night,
Tyler found out
that his new pajamas
were pretty cool,
too.